NICK JR. DORA the EXPLORER™

Dora Loves Boots

by Alison Inches
based on the teleplay "Best Friends" by Eric Weiner
illustrated by Zina Saunders

Toybox inc. Innovations

¡Hola! I'm Dora. Happy Valentine's Day! Valentine's Day is the perfect day to spend time with your friends. I'm going to spend it with my best friend, Boots.

Boots loves strawberries. Will you help me pick five yummy strawberries for his Valentine's Day surprise? Great! Let's count them in Spanish: *¡Uno, dos, tres, cuatro, cinco!* Good counting!

Boots and I are going to meet at Rainbow Rock. Will you help us both get there? Thanks!

It's me, Boots! I'm on my way to meet Dora at Rainbow Rock. I love spending time with my best friend, Dora—especially on Valentine's Day!

I'm going to bring Dora some chocolate from Chocolate Lake. Dora loves chocolate!

Boots and I both need to find a way to get to Rainbow Rock. Who do we ask for help when we don't know which way to go? That's right, the Map! Say "Map!"

Map says that I have to go through Valentine Gate.
Boots has to go past the Rosy Red Crabs. That's how we'll
both get to Rainbow Rock.

Will you help Boots get past the Rosy Red Crabs?

How am I going to get past all these Rosy Red Crabs?
I can't go under the crabs, so I have to go over them!
Do you see something I can use to swing over the crabs?

Yeah! I can use the vines. Here I come, Dora!

I need to go through Valentine Gate but it's locked.
Do you see the key? There it is! Uh-oh. I hear Swiper the fox!
I think that sneaky fox is trying to swipe the key. If you see
Swiper, say "Swiper, no swiping!"

Thanks! You stopped Swiper, and I made it through Valentine Gate. I can't wait to see Boots!

All right, I made it past the Rosy Red Crabs.
Now I can climb up Rainbow Rock.
   I'm on my way, Dora!

Boots and I are almost together. I need a rope, *una cuerda,* so I can climb to the top of Rainbow Rock. Let's check Backpack for a rope. Can you say "Backpack"? Great!

Do you see a rope? You found it! Thanks!

Oh, boy! Dora's almost here. I'm going to help her climb up Rainbow Rock.

Thanks for helping me, Boots. I made it to the top of Rainbow Rock! You're the best friend in the whole world. Here's a Valentine's Day surprise just for you!

Strawberries! I love strawberries!
Thanks, Dora! I have a Valentine's Day
surprise for you too.

Chocolate! I *love* chocolate! *¡Gracias, Boots!*

Mmmmm, we love strawberries and chocolate, but we love being together on Valentine's Day most of all. We couldn't have done it without your help. *¡Adiós!*

Happy Valentine's Day!